Visit us on the Web!
StepIntoReading.com
randomhousekids.com

Educators and librarians, for a variety of teaching tools, visit us at RHTeachersLibrarians.com

ISBN 978-0-399-55300-4

MANUFACTURED IN CHINA

10 9 8 7

STEP INTO READING®

nickelodeon

PAW PATROL™

FIVE PUPTACULAR TALES!

A Collection of Five
Step 1 and Step 2 Early Readers

Random House 🏠 New York

Contents

STEP INTO READING®

nickelodeon

Chase's Space Case

by Kristen L. Depken
illustrated by MJ Illustrations

Random House 🏠 New York

Ryder and the pups
are looking
at the stars.

They see a spaceship!

It is crashing!

Crash!

A space bubble comes
out of the ship.

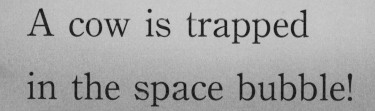

A cow is trapped
in the space bubble!

Mayor Goodway calls
the PAW Patrol
for help.

Ready for action!

Chase helps the cow.

Then he looks around.

A space alien has put
Mayor Goodway
in a bubble!

Chase helps.
Then he checks the farm
for the alien.

Melon.

Melon.

Space alien.

Melon.

Another bubble!

Zip!

Chase pulls
himself free.

The space alien is
in the Lookout!

He is trying
to fly the Lookout home!
He misses his mom.

The spaceship is back!

Rocky fixed it.

The space alien is happy!

The space alien gives
Ryder and the pups
a ride.

Best ride ever!

Ryder and the pups
wave goodbye
to their new friend.

nickelodeon

RUBBLE
TO THE
RESCUE!

PAW
PATROL

by Kristen L. Depken
illustrated by MJ Illustrations

Random House 🏠 New York

Rubble wants

to be a super pup!

Rubble wants
to help someone.

Farmer Yumi needs help.

Her chickens are loose!

Rubble the Super Pup
will help!

He gets all the chickens
into their pen.

Rubble finds
Mayor Goodway next.
She needs help!

There was a rockslide.
A train is stuck
in the tunnel!
The mayor needs
the PAW Patrol
to help.

Rubble runs
to the mountain.
"Where is the PAW Patrol?"
asks the engineer.

"Rubble the Super Pup
will save the day
his own way!"
says Rubble.

Rubble pushes the rocks.

More rocks fall!
Now both ends
of the tunnel
are blocked.

Rubble needs help.

He calls Ryder.

The PAW Patrol is on the way!

Zuma drives
Rubble's digger.

Chase moves a rock.
Rubble is free!

Rubble uses his digger
to move the other
rocks.

The train is free!
The engineer thanks
Ryder and the pups.

Rubble is happy
the team helped him.
They saved the day
the PAW Patrol way!

nickelodeon

CHASE IS ON THE CASE!

PAW PATROL

by Geof Smith

illustrated by Fabrizio Petrossi

Random House 🏠 New York

Ryder sees a problem
at the lighthouse.

The light is out.
Without it,
ships could crash
into Seal Island!

Captain Turbot calls
Ryder for help.

Captain Turbot cannot
find the lighthouse.
He is lost in the fog!

PAW Patrol is ready for action!

"We need to fix
the lighthouse,"
Ryder tells the pups.

"Chase, I need your searchlight," says Ryder.

"We will need
Zuma's hovercraft, too."

Ryder, Zuma, and Chase race to Seal Island.

"We have to fix
that light,"
says Ryder.

Wally the walrus
is in the way!
"He wants a treat,"
says Ryder.

He throws a treat.

"Catch, Wally!"

Wally gulps it down.

Ryder, Zuma, and Chase
reach Seal Island.
A big ship is coming!

Chase is
on the case!
He will warn
the ship.

The lighthouse door
is locked!
Chase shoots out
his net.

Ryder climbs up the net.
Now he can go through
the window
and unlock the door.

Chase is in!
He turns on
his searchlight.

The big ship sees
Chase's light.
It turns away
from the rocks.
The ship is safe!

Captain Turbot follows
Chase's light.
He takes a new bulb
to the lighthouse.

The light is bright.

The lighthouse is fixed.

The PAW Patrol has

saved the day!

"Whenever you are
in trouble,
just yelp for help!"
Ryder says.

nickelodeon

PIT CREW PUPS

PAW PATROL

by Kristen L. Depken
illustrated by MJ Illustrations

Random House 🏠 New York

Alex is a friend
of the PAW Patrol.
He builds
a Super Trike.

He wants
to go super fast!
He shows
his grandpa.

Alex puts on
his helmet.

Alex pedals.

The trike falls apart!

The parts go

everywhere!

Who can help?
The PAW Patrol!
Alex's grandpa
calls Ryder.

The pups are ready
to help.
Here they come!

Chase directs traffic.

Ryder and Alex pick up

the trike parts.

Rocky brings the parts
to the garage.
He and Ryder
put the trike
back together.

Alex's Super Trike
is even better
than before.

Alex is ready

to go super fast.

Ryder tells him to wait.

But Alex zooms off.

Alex speeds
down a hill.
He goes too fast.
He cannot stop!

The pups chase
after him.
He races toward
the busy street!

Chase stops
the traffic
just in time.

Alex and Ryder zoom

onto a bridge.

Ryder calls Skye.
She flies her helicopter
over the bridge.
She spots Alex and
hooks on to his trike.

The trike stops!
Alex is safe.

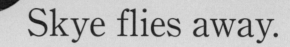

Skye flies away.

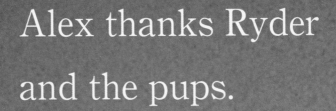

Alex thanks Ryder
and the pups.

Next time,
he will slow down.

Ryder and the pups
take Alex
to get lemonade.

The pups show Alex
how to ride safely.

Ryder gives Alex

a prize for

safe driving.

Hooray for Alex!

nickelodeon

PAW PATROL

KING for a DAY!

by Mary Tillworth
illustrated by MJ Illustrations

Random House 🏠 New York

The PAW Patrol pups
are in a play.

They wear costumes.

Chase is the king.
The other pups
are knights.

Captain Turbot builds
a castle for the play.
He hammers
one last nail.

The castle falls!

Captain Turbot is stuck.

He calls the

PAW Patrol for help.

Ryder and his pups
race to the rescue!

They are ready
to help Captain Turbot.

Rubble lifts

the castle wall.

Chase pulls

the castle tower

off the captain.

Marshall x-rays
Captain Turbot.
Whew!

No broken bones!

Now the pups
must fix the castle.
Skye flies a wall
into place.

Rocky screws a door onto the wall.

Marshall and Ryder

paint the castle.

The castle is finished!

The play can start.

Chase begins to cough.

Marshall checks him out.
Chase is sick!

Ryder asks Marshall
to play the king.

The play begins.

A princess is trapped
in the tower.

A king must save her.

The pup who can
pull the bone
from the stone
will become king!

Marshall tries.

He pulls the bone.

It hits the tower!

The princess falls
from the tower!

Marshall catches

the princess!

What a good pup!

Lady Skye puts a crown
on Marshall's head.

Hooray!

The king saved the day.

And Marshall saved

the play!